The Wizard of Oz

L. Frank Baum

Retold by Rosie Dickins

Illustrated by Mauro Evangelista

Reading consultant: Alison Kelly
Roehampton University

Contents

Chapter 1
The cyclone 3

Chapter 2
A scarecrow, a tinman and a lion 9

Chapter 3
A dangerous journey 17

Chapter 4
Emerald City 24

Chapter 5
The Wicked Witch 33

Chapter 6
The wizard's trick 44

Chapter 7
Oz's rewards 53

Chapter 8
Home again 58

Chapter 1

The cyclone

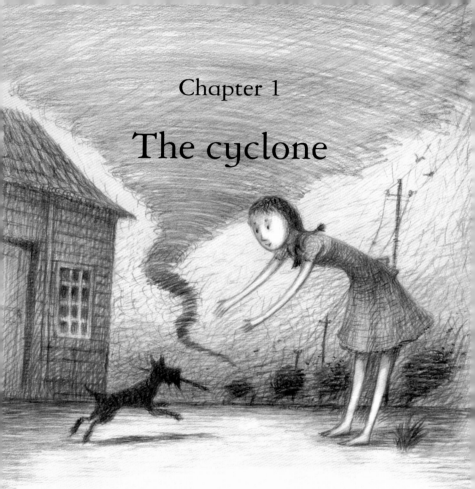

Dorothy lived on a lonely farm in Kansas, with only her Uncle Henry, her Aunt Em and her little dog Toto for company. One day, as they played outside, the sky grew dark...

Then the wind whipped up, with a chilling moan.

"There's a cyclone coming," called her Uncle Henry. "Quick, into the cellar!"

In a panic, Toto ran to hide under her bed. Dorothy dashed after him, as the wind shrieked and the whole house shook.

With a mighty wrench, the
cyclone whirled the house into the
sky. Dorothy shivered with terror.
  "What will happen to us Toto?"
she whispered.

The house sailed through the sky for hours... Suddenly, with a sickening jolt, they landed.

"Welcome to Oz," cried a man in a pointed hat, "and thank you! You've just killed the Wicked Witch of the East and set us free."

"Who? What?" asked Dorothy, horrified. "I haven't killed anyone."

"Well, your house did," a woman told her. "Look!" Two scrawny legs stuck out from under a wall.

As Dorothy looked,
the legs vanished, leaving only a
pair of silvery shoes behind. The
woman handed them to Dorothy.

"These are yours now," she said.

7

Dorothy took the shoes in a daze. "Do you know the way to Kansas?" she asked. "I have to go home."

The strangers shook their heads.

"Maybe the Great Wizard can help," suggested the woman. "He lives in Emerald City, at the end of the yellow brick road..."

Chapter 2

A scarecrow, a tinman and a lion

Emerald City

Dorothy packed some food and set out for the city at once. She walked briskly along the yellow road, her silver shoes tinkling on the bricks.

9

As she passed a field, a scarecrow winked at her. Dorothy jumped in surprise.

"How do you do?" he asked.

"He talks too!" thought Dorothy. "H-hello," she said, shyly. "How are you?"

"Not so good," the scarecrow said. "It's very boring stuck up here..."

"Where are you off to?" he asked, a moment later.

"To see the wizard," Dorothy replied. "I need help to get home."

"Wizard? What wizard?" said the scarecrow. "I don't know anything," he added sadly. "I have no brains."

"Oh dear," said Dorothy. "Well, why don't you come with me?"

Maybe the wizard could give you some brains.

So they went on together. The land grew wilder until, by evening, they were walking through a thick forest. That night, they sheltered in a log cabin.

Dorothy woke to hear strange groans. A man made of tin was standing, as still as a statue, by a pile of logs.

"Are you alright?" she asked.

"No!" the tinman grunted. "I can't move. I was caught in the rain and I've rusted."

Dorothy spotted an oil can and swiftly oiled the tinman's joints.

"Thank you," he sighed. "I might have stood there forever. What brings you here?"

"The scarecrow and I are going to see the Great Wizard," Dorothy told him. "I want to go home and the scarecrow wants a brain."

The tinman thought for a second. "Do you think the wizard could give me a heart?" he asked.

"I expect so," said Dorothy.

"Then I'll come too," he decided. The new companions had just set off when a lion leaped onto the road. Opening his slobbery jaws, he gave a terrible roar.

As the lion towered over Toto, Dorothy smacked him on the nose.

"Stop it!" she cried. "You must be a coward to pick on a little dog."

The lion looked ashamed. "You're right," he mumbled. "I only roar to make people run away."

"You should ask the wizard for courage," said Dorothy and told him where they were going.

The lion nodded eagerly. "I'll come with you!" he growled.

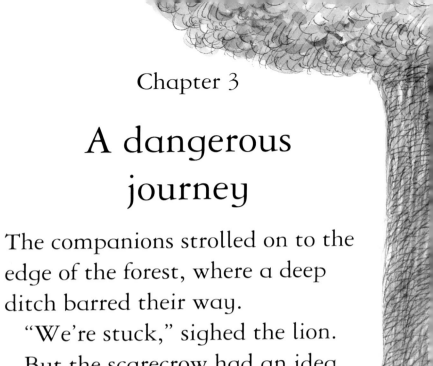

Chapter 3

A dangerous journey

The companions strolled on to the edge of the forest, where a deep ditch barred their way.

"We're stuck," sighed the lion.

But the scarecrow had an idea. "If the tinman chops down this tree, we could use it to cross the ditch."

The tree made a perfect bridge. They were almost across when they heard fierce growls from behind.

"A tiger monster!" whimpered the lion. "We're all doomed..."

"Quick tinman!" ordered the scarecrow. "Chop away the tree."

The tree bridge fell with a
crash and the monster plummeted
into the ditch. Dorothy and her
friends hurried on. Soon, they
arrived at a broad river.

"We need a raft," declared the
scarecrow and the tinman set to
work once again.

The raft bobbed along happily until they reached the middle of the river. Here, the current was so strong, it swept them away.

The lion dived in, took hold of the raft and swam as hard as he could. Slowly, he pulled them ashore.

Safely over the river, they went on, through a field bursting with poppies. A spicy scent filled the air and Dorothy felt drowsy. She sank into the flowers and wouldn't wake.

"It's the poppies..." yawned the lion. "They've sent... her... to sleep."

Luckily, the tinman and the scarecrow – who weren't made of flesh – stayed wide awake.

"Run!" the scarecrow ordered the lion. "We'll bring Dorothy."

The lion bounded ahead, leaving the scarecrow and tinman to carry Dorothy and Toto from the field.

On and on the pair staggered. Almost at the end of the poppies they passed the lion – fast asleep.

Quickly, they laid Dorothy in the open air to recover and went back. With much pushing and pulling, grunting and groaning, they dragged the lion to safety.

Chapter 4

Emerald City

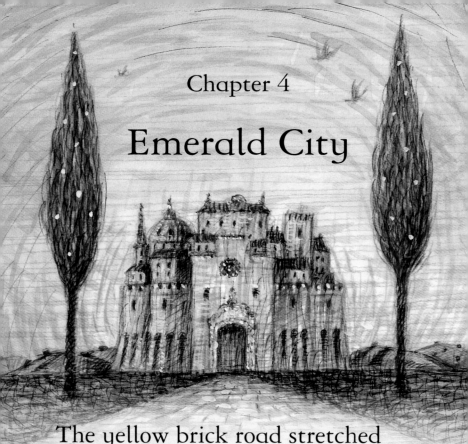

The yellow brick road stretched
off into the distance, but on the
horizon, something sparkled. Soon,
a vast green city loomed ahead.

"We've made it!" said Dorothy.

"Look," added the lion, pointing
to a gate studded with emeralds.

24

Dorothy knocked on the gate and a man in a green uniform appeared.
"Yes?" he said.
"Please may we see the Great Wizard?" asked Dorothy.

"I can take you to his palace," said the man, "but you must wear glasses. Our city is dazzling." And he pulled out a pair of green glasses for each of them, including Toto.

25

Inside, the city was an incredible sight. The streets and houses were built of shining green marble and all the people wore green. The shops sold green popcorn, green hats and green shoes. Everything was green – even the sky.

The gatekeeper led them to a grand palace.

"We'd like to see the wizard," Dorothy told the soldier on guard.

"Enter one at a time," he barked. "You first."

Nervously, Dorothy went inside.
"I am the wizard," boomed a
giant head. "Why do you seek me?"

Dorothy took a deep breath. "Can
you send me home to Kansas?"

The head frowned. "Only if you
do something for me first," it
snapped. "Kill the Wicked Witch
of the West. Now go!"

Then the scarecrow stepped in.
A lady with green wings was
sitting on the throne. "I am the
wizard," she said gently. "What
do you seek?"

"I am only a scarecrow, stuffed
with straw. I ask you for brains."

First, kill the Wicked Witch of the West. Now go!

Whatever you want, you must first kill the Wicked Witch of the West!

The tinman saw a terrible beast with five eyes and five limbs.

"I am the wizard," roared the beast. "Why do you seek me?"

"I am made of tin and have no heart. Please give me a heart, so I can love and be happy," he begged. But he too was turned away.

The lion went last. Now, above the throne, blazed a ball of fire.

"I am the wizard," hissed the ball. "Why do you seek me?"

"I am a c-c-coward," stammered the lion. "I want c-c-courage, so I may truly be King of the Beasts."

First, kill the Wicked Witch of the West. Now go!

Outside the palace, the friends were glum. "We can't defeat a witch," moaned the scarecrow.

"But we can try," said the lion. So they walked back to the gate.

"Good luck," said the gatekeeper, pointing out the path to the witch's castle. "You'll need it!"

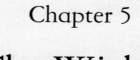

Chapter 5

The Wicked Witch

The Wicked Witch of the West had only one eye, but it saw a long way. She spotted the friends as they left the city. "Strangers coming here?" she screeched. She blew a whistle and a pack of wolves ran up. "Tear the strangers to shreds," she said.

The wolves bared their teeth and
dashed away. Luckily, the tinman
heard them coming.

As the first
wolf reached them,
he chopped off its head. Again and
again he swung his hatchet, until
all the wolves lay dead.

34

The witch scowled. She blew her whistle twice and a flock of crows flew down. "Peck the strangers to pieces," she snapped.

This time, the scarecrow saw them coming. As the first crow flew at him, the scarecrow grabbed him and wrung his neck. One by one, he wrung the neck of every single crow.

Now the witch was furious. She blew three times on her whistle to fetch a swarm of bees. "Sting the strangers to death!" she screamed.

Quickly, the scarecrow scattered straw over Dorothy, Toto and the lion to hide them. The bees tried to attack the tinman instead, but they snapped their stingers on his hard, tin body and died.

The witch gnashed her teeth, but she had one last trick up her sleeve – a cap which gave its owner three wishes. The witch had one wish left.

As she put on the cap, a crowd of magic monkeys appeared in a rush of wings. "Kill the strangers!" she howled. "Except the lion. I want him as my slave."

The monkeys flew off and seized the friends. They pulled out the scarecrow's stuffing and dropped him in the trees. They threw the tinman onto a rocky plain, smashing him to pieces. And they tied up the lion to carry him to the castle.

But at Dorothy, they stopped. "We can't hurt her," they said. "Let's take her to the witch."

Dorothy didn't know it, but the silver shoes gave her great power. The witch gulped when she saw them... until she noticed how frightened Dorothy was.

"She doesn't know about the shoes!" the witch thought gleefully, and set Dorothy to work.

The lion was tied up outside. Dorothy couldn't see how they would ever escape. Every way out was guarded by the witch's slaves.

But the witch had lost much of her power. "My wolves, my crows, my bees... all dead," she thought angrily. "Even my cap has no more wishes left. Well, I must steal those silver shoes."

I need a plan...

Silently, the witch put an invisible
iron bar on the ground. Dorothy
tripped over it and one of her shoes
flew off. The witch pounced on it.

"Give me back my shoe," said
Dorothy crossly.

"Never," cackled the witch. "And
I shall steal the other one too!"

Dorothy was so angry she threw a pail of water over the witch. At once, the witch began to shrink.

"Agh! I'm melting..." she wailed.

Soon, all that was left of the witch was a brown puddle and one silver shoe. Dorothy hastily put her shoe back on and raced out to the lion.

"The witch is dead!" she shouted.

Chapter 6

The wizard's trick

The witch's slaves danced with joy and helped Dorothy and the lion look for their friends. It didn't take long to find the battered remains of the scarecrow and the tinman.

We're free!

The tinman was soon put back together and after the scarecrow had been stuffed with fresh straw, he felt as good as new.

"Now," said Dorothy, "let's go and claim our rewards!" So they packed her basket with food from the witch's kitchen, covered it with a cloth cap and set off.

After several hours, they stopped for lunch. "I can't wait to see the wizard," said Dorothy, as she unpacked the basket.

I wish we were in Emerald City!

There was a fluttering of wings and, to everyone's surprise, the magic monkeys appeared.

All at once, the friends were
flying through the air. Before long,
they could see the shining roofs of
Emerald City. The monkeys set
them down, bowed and flew away.

The wizard kept them waiting
for ages. Finally, a soldier with a
green beard ushered them in.

47

This time, the room was empty, but a voice echoed, "I am the wizard. Why do you seek me?"

"To claim our rewards," said the friends. "The Wicked Witch is dead."

"But..." began the voice.

"We want our rewards!" roared the lion. Toto jumped in fright and knocked over a screen in the corner...

...to reveal a little old man, with fuzzy hair and glasses.

"Who are you?" demanded the tinman, waving his hatchet.

"I'm the wizard," croaked the man. "But you can call me Oz."

"What about the head – the lady – the beast – the ball of fire?" cried the friends.

"Um, they were tricks," Oz said, sheepishly. "I'm not a real wizard. I'm not even from here. I was in a hot-air balloon that blew off-course. Since I appeared from the sky, the people thought I was a wizard."

"They asked me to rule them and I built Emerald City. Isn't it green?" Oz asked proudly. "Of course, you have to wear green-tinted glasses for the full effect," he admitted.

"The witches were my only fear. I was so glad when your house killed the first one. I would have said anything to get rid of the other."

"But what about our rewards?"
asked the friends together.

"You don't need them," Oz
replied. "Scarecrow, you're full of
ideas. Lion, you're brave, you just
lack confidence. And tinman, hearts
make most people unhappy."

"But you promised!" they said.

Oz sighed. "I'll do my best."

Can you send me home to Kansas?

I'll try.

Chapter 7

Oz's rewards

Oz summoned everyone the very next day. "Scarecrow first," he said.

He took the scarecrow's head and tipped in a handful of pins. "This will make you as sharp as a pin!"

And the scarecrow felt very wise.

Next came the tinman. "Here's your heart," Oz said, giving him a heart-shaped cushion. "It's a very kind one." The tinman beamed.

Then Oz produced a green bottle. "This is courage," he told the lion.

The lion gulped it down. "Now I feel brave!" he roared.

Finally, Oz led Dorothy to a basket. "I mended my balloon," he said.

We'll fly home!

He lit a fire and hot air swelled the balloon. The basket began to lift. "Hurry!" Oz cried to Dorothy – but she was looking for Toto. She swept him up and ran to the basket.

Just as she reached it, a rope
snapped and the balloon took off.
"Come back!" she called.

It was too late. "Now I'll never
get home," she wept. Her friends
hated to see her so unhappy. The
scarecrow racked his new brains.

"I know," he said. "Wish for the magic monkeys to take you!"

But they couldn't help. "We can't leave this land," they explained.

Then a soldier spoke up. "Why not ask the Good Witch Glinda?"

So Dorothy and her friends set off once more.

Chapter 8

Home again

Glinda lived far in the south. It would have been a difficult journey without the cap's third wish.

"Please take us to Glinda," said Dorothy and the monkeys carried them to a beautiful castle.

"What can I do for you?" Glinda asked her visitors kindly.

Dorothy told her the whole story. "And now I just want to go home," she finished.

"Bless you," said Glinda, smiling. "I'm sure I can get you all home. But I'll need the wishing cap."

She turned to the others. "What will you do when Dorothy leaves?"

"I'll live in Emerald City," the scarecrow told her.

"I'll go back to my cabin," said the tinman.

"And I'll go home to the forest," added the lion.

"I'll ask the monkeys to take you all where you wish," said Glinda. "Then I'll set them free."

"You're very kind," said Dorothy, "but please, how can I get home?"

"Your silver shoes will take you," replied Glinda. "Just knock the heels together three times and say where you want to go."

With glistening eyes,
Dorothy said goodbye to
her friends. Then she hugged
Toto tightly and clicked her heels
together. "Take me home!"
she cried.

At once, she was whirling
through the air... and rolling on
the soft grass of a familiar field.

Aunt Em dropped her watering can and rushed over. "My darling child!" she said, covering Dorothy with kisses. "Wherever did you come from?"

"From Oz," said Dorothy. "And oh, Aunt Em, I'm so glad to be home!"

L. Frank Baum grew up in a wealthy American family. He had several jobs before becoming a writer, including running a store and breeding chickens. But he always loved telling stories – and people loved reading them. "The Wizard of Oz" was an instant hit when it was published, sparking off a whole series of books set in Oz, as well as a famous film.

Series editor: Lesley Sims
Designed by Katarina Dragoslavic

First published in 2006 by Usborne Publishing Ltd.,
Usborne House, 83-85 Saffron Hill, London EC1N 8RT, England.
www.usborne.com